QUICKREADS

THE VERY BAD DREAM

ANNE SCHRAFF

SADDLEBACK
EDUCATIONAL PUBLISHING

QUICKREADS

SERIES 1

Black Widow Beauty
Danger on Ice
Empty Eyes
The Experiment
The Kula'i Street Knights
The Mystery Quilt
No Way to Run
The Ritual
The 75-Cent Son
The Very Bad Dream

SERIES 2

The Accuser
Ben Cody's Treasure
Blackout
The Eye of the Hurricane
The House on the Hill
Look to the Light
Ring of Fear
The Tiger Lily Code
Tug-of-War
The White Room

SERIES 3

The Bad Luck Play
Breaking Point
Death Grip
Fat Boy
No Exit
No Place Like Home
The Plot
Something Dreadful Down Below
Sounds of Terror
The Woman Who Loved a Ghost

SERIES 4

The Barge Ghost
Beasts
Blood and Basketball
Bus 99
The Dark Lady
Dimes to Dollars
Read My Lips
Ruby's Terrible Secret
Student Bodies
Tough Girl

SADDLEBACK
EDUCATIONAL PUBLISHING
www.sdlback.com

ISBN-13: 978-1-61651-187-6
ISBN-10: 1-61651-187-7
eBook: 978-1-60291-909-9

Printed in Guangzhou, China
0311/03-150-11

15 14 13 12 11   2 3 4 5 6

■ ■ ■

Valerie Monroe had never had such a bad dream in her life! Maybe it had something to do with the scary stuff she'd been studying in her criminal justice class. Or maybe she'd eaten some bad food at dinner on her Saturday night date with her boyfriend, Clay Turman.

On Sunday, at the beach with Clay, Valerie talked about the dream. "All day it's been replaying in my mind like a horror movie. And the worst part of it is that you were in it!"

Clay nibbled on his hot dog sandwich. "Forget it," he said. "I don't obsess on stuff like that."

"But, Clay—in my dream, you were carrying this burlap sack with a *body* inside!

You had a pick with you so you could bury it. I actually watched you bury a body in Cougar Canyon!" Valerie groaned.

"How do you know there was a body in the bag?" Clay asked off-handedly.

"Oh, Clay—I saw the blood! And the shape looked just like a body," Valerie said in a shaky whisper.

"Ewww!" Clay laughed in a silly, teasing way.

"Come on, Clay, don't joke about it! It isn't funny. Why would I have had such a horrible dream?" Valerie asked.

Clay shrugged. "Who knows where dreams come from? It might have been the calamari we had at Rocky's Fish House. Mixing squid with booze will do it every time," he chuckled.

Clay was a tall, good-looking guy with lots of friends, many of them girls. He was considered a real hunk. That's why Valerie felt flattered when he'd asked her out a few months ago. Since then they had been dating regularly.

■ ■ ■

After Valerie got home on Sunday, she told her roommate, Amy Faulk, about the nightmare. Amy shook her head and said, "Has to be all that gory stuff you're learning in college. It must be seeping into your dreams."

"But, Amy, do you think dreams like that *mean* anything?" Valerie asked. "It all seemed so *real!*"

Amy continued painting her toenails. Without looking up, she said, "I read once that dreams are usually based on stuff that already happened. But I've also heard that dreams sometimes tell us about the future."

Valerie flipped on the evening news. The city council was arguing about whether or not to build a new ball park. Then the lady news anchor's face turned grim. "Now, here's the latest on the body that was discovered early this morning in Cougar Canyon."

Valerie felt the room darken. She gripped the arms of her chair. "Amy!" she screamed.

"Don't freak out," Amy cried, rushing over to Valerie. "Can't you see what happened? This explains everything! You got home from your date with Clay after midnight, right? You must have turned on the radio and heard them talking about the body in Cougar Canyon. Then you fell asleep and just *dreamed* it, girl!"

Valerie felt weak with relief. "Of course!" she cried. "I just incorporated poor Clay into the dream. Then I forgot that I'd heard it on the radio."

"Look!" Amy said. "Your scream made me mess up my toenail polish. Now I have to start all over again!"

After a day or so, the name of the victim in Cougar Canyon came out. It was a 22-year-old waitress named Bonnie Lewis. She was single, living just a few blocks from the apartment Valerie and Amy shared.

The next morning Valerie looked at the dead girl's picture in the paper. "Look, Amy. She was pretty. She sorta looks like me, doesn't she?"

"She and her boyfriend probably had a big argument, and he lost his head and killed her," Amy surmised.

In her criminal justice class the next day, Valerie started talking about the murder with a classmate, Brad Duncan. Brad was entering the police academy in the fall.

"Want to hear something weird?" Valerie began. Then she started telling Brad all about her strange dream.

"Wow, that *is* weird!" Brad agreed.

As Valerie glanced at the newspaper article, she noticed that Bonnie Lewis had worked at Sammy's Pancake House. "Hey, I've eaten there," Valerie said. "It's right across from the muffler shop where my boyfriend works. I wonder if Bonnie ever waited on me when I was there."

After class, Valerie began to brood about the bad dream again. Clay worked across the street from Sammy's. Had he known Bonnie Lewis?

Valerie drove over to the muffler shop and saw Clay working on a pickup truck. When he saw her come in, he looked up and grinned. "Hey, babe, what're you doing here?"

Valerie was clutching the newspaper article about the murdered girl. "Clay, that girl they found murdered in Cougar Canyon—she worked at Sammy's, right across the street." Valerie held up the photo of Bonnie. "Did you ever see her over there?"

The smile disappeared from Clay's face. He seemed annoyed. "What is this with you, Val? You still harping on that stupid dream? Look—I never saw the chick before, okay?"

Rocky Penn, another man who worked in the muffler shop, heard the conversation and walked over. He smirked and said, "I remember that girl. You should too, Clay. When you tried to hit on her, she put you down."

Laughing as if he'd just told a good joke, Rocky went back to his work. Clay's eyes went hard, and he glared at the other man's back with naked hatred.

■ ■ ■

As Valerie walked back to her Escort, Clay followed her. "Hey, Valerie, I'm sorry I was kinda rude just now. But your dream is getting on my nerves. And Rocky never misses a chance to stick it to me. I'm having a really bad day."

"Yeah, sure," Valerie said.

Valerie stopped at a coffee shop to think. On Saturday night, she and Clay had gone to dinner and then on to a couple of nightclubs. Usually, she drank only moderately—and she *thought* she was doing that on Saturday. But by the time she'd gotten home she was wobbly on her feet! In fact, Clay had to hold her up until she got inside her apartment.

Valerie remembered dashing cold water on her face to sober up and then going to bed. Obviously, she must have heard about the dead girl while listening to the radio and then dreamed about her.

Valerie had another cup of black coffee. Every time she thought about the bad dream, it gave her fresh chills. The scene was so realistic!

That evening, Valerie had a movie date with Clay. She didn't feel much like going, but she didn't want to stand him up, either. When Clay showed up at her apartment, he said, "I talked to the police today."

Valerie stiffened. "Really, Clay? How come?" she said.

"They're questioning all the guys who even remotely knew that Lewis woman. I guess she must have waited on me a couple times," Clay said. He cleared his throat and said, "Rocky lied, Valerie. I never hit on her. Uh—you haven't talked to the cops, have you?" he asked with obvious nervousness.

"Why should I?" Valerie asked in surprise.

"Oh, you know—to tell them that stupid dream stuff," Clay said.

Valerie shook her head. "But that reminds me, Clay. How come I seemed to get so drunk that night? I don't remember having very many drinks."

Clay looked surprised and amused. "Oh,

yeah, you were really going for those martinis, babe." He grinned at her. "Don't you remember *anything* about Saturday night?"

"Not much," Valerie said. "Just that I felt really drunk when we were coming home."

"Well, just forget about it, Val. It's all over now," Clay said. "Let's go out now and enjoy the movie."

"Sure," Valerie said, but for some reason she had the shivers. Why did Clay seem so anxious about her memories of Saturday night?

■ ■ ■

Amy," Valerie said to her roommate after she came home from the movie date, "was I really smashed when I got home Saturday night?"

Amy raised her eyebrows. "Kinda. And your smarty boyfriend was really upset." Amy had never liked Clay Turman. She didn't trust him.

"Amy, what if it *wasn't* a dream?" Valerie asked in a shaky voice. "What if I was asleep in the car, and I *saw*—you know—Clay carrying this dead girl?"

Amy looked shocked. "You're kidding, right?"

"No, I'm not. I'm just so scared. I'm confused and scared," Valerie said.

"Val, if you think you actually saw a crime, then you'd better talk to the police," Amy said sternly.

"But, Amy—what if it *was* just a crazy dream? Then I'd be getting Clay into terrible trouble over nothing! How can I do that to him?" Valerie wailed.

"On the other hand," Amy pointed out, "if Clay Turman murdered that girl, maybe *you're* next. Have you ever thought about that?"

Valerie couldn't sleep that night. In the morning she rushed to her criminal justice class. She could only remember bits and pieces of that fateful Saturday night. She remembered eating at The Dock, then dancing at the Zodiac Club. After that, she remembered going on to a place called

Skippy's. But she didn't remember what happened there.

Before class started, Valerie told Brad Duncan that she was still very uneasy about her dream.

"Hey, Val—are you like a psychic or something?" Brad asked. "Has anything like this ever happened to you before?"

"No. I guess I just heard the report on the radio early Sunday morning. I must have built my dream out of that," Valerie said.

"No, Valerie," Brad said with a serious look on his face. "My dad's in the police department. He told me that the first news reports on the murder were released on Sunday *afternoon.*"

"Are you sure?" Valerie cried.

"Yeah, I'm sure," Brad said. "Valerie, are you okay?"

"Oh, yeah," Valerie mumbled. But her mind was spinning. Brad suddenly grasped her hand. "Look, we're just school buddies— but I do care about you. If anything comes up and you need a shoulder to lean on, here's my

cell phone number and my pager number."
Brad slipped a card into Valerie's hand.

After class, Valerie called Clay on her cell
phone. "We need to meet at a coffee shop to
talk," she said tensely.

Clay seemed to sense the gravity in
Valerie's voice. "All right, how about
Patilonia's in ten minutes? Is that okay?"

"Okay," Valerie said. Cold chills ran up
and down her spine. Suddenly she was
feeling afraid of Clay Turman.

■ ■ ■

Clay was waiting for Valerie in a back
booth. He must have driven over to the coffee
shop in a big hurry.

"Clay, I want you to tell me the truth about
Saturday night," Valerie said. "What really
happened?"

This time, Clay didn't try to make light
of the dream. He looked grim. "I hoped we'd
never have to talk about it," he said. "It was
a terrible accident."

"Tell me, Clay! I really need to know

what happened," Valerie said, feeling numb and sick.

"Let's take a walk," Clay said.

They walked down the street together. Valerie was glad there were enough people around to make her feel safe, but no one was close enough to overhear their conversation.

"Okay, Clay—so tell me about the accident," Valerie said.

"Well, we were hitting the bars, and you had gotten pretty tanked, babe. Unfortunately, we ran into Bonnie Lewis at Jimmy's, the last place we hit. She came on to me and you got mad. She started yelling and calling you names. The next thing I knew you got hold of that iron lock bar for the steering wheel. Then you—you whacked her," Clay said.

Valerie could scarcely breathe. *What are you saying?"* She cried out.

"You swung the bar at her, and it cracked her skull, babe," Clay said.

"Clay, that's *insane!"* Valerie cried.

Clay ignored her. "Well, I could see the chick was dead. But there was nobody in the parking lot. So I stuffed Bonnie in some burlap sacks I had in my trunk. Then I headed for Cougar Canyon. I knew it was an accident. You didn't mean to hurt her. Why should my girl go to prison for an accident?"

"No, Clay! I would *remember* if I had killed somebody!" Valerie said.

"Listen—the cops will never pin it on you. It'll just be one more unsolved crime. Bonnie Lewis was just a cheap chick, anyway. You're in the clear, babe. No sweat," Clay said.

"But Clay, I *didn't* hurt that girl," Valerie insisted.

"You were drunk. Blind drunk. Look, Val, I covered it all up to protect you. I did it because I love you," Clay reached out to grasp Valerie's hand.

Valerie wrenched free of him. "You're lying!" she cried.

Clay's expression darkened. "Look, Valerie—if you go to the cops about what you saw in your stupid dream, I'll tell them what you did. It's all gonna blow up in your own pretty little face. You'll be wearing ugly prison dresses until you're old and gray!"

■ ■ ■

Valerie felt like a zombie as she drove home. Her mind was spinning out of control. She knew she didn't hit that girl the way Clay said she did. Valerie wasn't a violent person. She hadn't struck another human being since she hit another toddler with a teddy bear.

But Clay probably had Valerie's fingerprints on the iron bar. All he would have had to do was to hand it to her on Saturday night. After that, it would be Clay's word against hers.

Valerie wanted desperately to talk her problem over with someone—but who? On weekends she usually had dinner with her parents. But it would only make things worse to worry them.

Maybe, Valerie thought, Clay had put a mind-altering substance in her drink Saturday night. Then he'd had an argument with Bonnie Lewis, struck and killed her, and finally hidden the body. Valerie was probably half-asleep in the car when it happened. But she was just awake enough to see him carrying Bonnie's body to that shallow grave in Cougar Canyon.

Valerie was terrified. What if she was accused of murdering Bonnie Lewis? What if she fell apart during the police questioning? That could make her look guilty. Or what if the police decided that Valerie and Clay were in it together and arrested *both* of them for murder?

Valerie struggled to pull herself together, to calm down. She tried to form a logical plan. Maybe if she went to Skippy's again, she could find someone there who had seen something. Maybe someone saw Clay arguing with Bonnie. Or maybe someone saw Valerie sleeping in the car in the parking lot while Clay and Bonnie argued.

Valerie sighed. If there was only someone she could turn to, someone she could trust! Then Brad's face came to mind. He'd offered to help, hadn't he?

But could Brad Duncan be trusted to look out for Valerie's best interests? After all, he was the son of a police officer who was working on the Lewis murder case. He himself was studying to be a cop. If Valerie told him everything, maybe he'd just go right to the phone and call the police.

But Valerie knew she couldn't go it alone. She was too scared. So she dug the card from her purse and punched in Brad's number.

"Valerie?" Brad answered, as if he had been expecting her call.

"Brad, I need help—bad. Do you know where Skippy's nightclub is?"

"Yes," he said.

"Could you please meet me there in ten minutes?" she asked.

"You got it," he said. "I'll be right there."

■ ■ ■

Skippy's was a medium-sized club. Around seven in the evening it filled up with young working people who came there to socialize and dance. Clay didn't like to dance, so that night they had just sipped their drinks at a table.

Valerie saw Brad at the bar when she walked in to Skippy's. He ordered two ginger ales and they sat down.

Then, taking a deep breath, she told him everything.

"Wow!" Brad said. "When you first told me about that dream I wondered if there was more to the story."

"You know, I really *did* think it was a dream at first," Valerie said.

Brad was looking intently at Valerie. She didn't know what to make of it. Was he wondering how to tell her that she would soon be under arrest? Did he believe she could actually have hit the other girl with the iron bar? After all, he didn't know her very well.

"Believe me, Brad—I'd never in a million years hurt anybody," Valerie said, "not even if I was drunk."

"Valerie, you know we'll have to call the

police, don't you?" Brad finally said.

Chills ran down Valerie's spine. So he was a cop first and a friend second. It was just as she had feared. Tears ran down her cheeks. "Oh, Brad, I can't face being arrested!" she cried out.

Brad reached across the table and covered Valerie's hands with his. "You won't be arrested," he said.

"How can you be so sure, Brad? Clay said that *my* fingerprints are on the iron bar," Valerie wailed.

"I can't say much about the case because my father is working on it, Val. But I *can* tell you this—Bonnie Lewis did not die from a blow. I can't tell you more than that," Brad said.

Valerie gasped. "Oh, Brad, do you mean it? Then I *couldn't* have killed her! Clay told me that just to keep me quiet!"

"I'm calling my father right now. Then I'll go down to the police station with you. You can tell the whole story there, Valerie," Brad said.

Valerie felt numb. She was *so* relieved that she wouldn't be a suspect in the case! But now she feared something else. Would the police catch Clay before he caught up with her?

■ ■ ■

Brad Duncan sat with Valerie as she told her story. But when the police went to Clay Turman's house to make an arrest, the man was gone.

"Valerie, I don't think it's safe for you to go back to your apartment," Brad said. "Not until Turman is in custody. Is there anywhere you can go that Turman doesn't know about?"

"My parents live about eight miles from here. Clay's never been to their house. I could go and stay there. But first I have to go to my apartment and get my things," Valerie said.

"Okay," Brad said. "Why don't I follow you to your place? I'll make sure you're okay while you pack."

"It's awfully nice of you to help me out like this," Valerie said gratefully.

"No problem," Brad said with a smile. He was very handsome when he smiled. Valerie wondered why she'd never noticed that before.

Brad followed Valerie to her place. He waited inside while she packed an overnight bag.

"All set," Valerie said to herself when she threw the last pair of shorts and T-shirt into the bag.

Before Brad drove off, Valerie gave him her parents' phone number, and he made sure she still had his cell number.

"Thanks again," Valerie said. "You've been a really good friend."

Brad watched while Valerie drove down the street and turned off on the freeway onramp.

Valerie's parents lived in a small bedroom community nestled in the foothills. It was the same two-story Tudor house where Valerie and her older sister had grown up. Just thinking of the family home filled Valerie with a flood of good memories—

family barbecues, basketball games at the garage door, and mom's chicken paprika.

Then Valerie noticed a car following her. The high-beam headlights were beginning to annoy her. She glanced into the rearview mirror and turned cold. It was Clay Turman's SUV!

Valerie gripped the steering wheel and tried to remain calm. She reached over for her cell phone and punched in Brad's number. She waited while it rang.

"Hi," Brad said.

"Help me, Brad! I'm on the interstate and Clay Turman is behind me," Valerie cried. "I'm so scared."

"Keep cool, Valerie! Keep going until you get to a well-lighted place with a lot of people around. I'll get help to you as soon as I can," Brad said.

Valerie told Brad just where she was, but she kept on going. She knew of a big drive-in restaurant about a half-mile away. Her plan was to leave the interstate there and drive into the brightly lit restaurant parking lot.

The SUV was right behind her as she headed for the restaurant. Then suddenly, Clay Turman gunned his engine and roared alongside Valerie's little car. Then he sideswiped it and knocked it onto the shoulder of the road! Valerie's cell phone flew to the floor.

Valerie was only about 100 yards from the restaurant, but her car's engine wouldn't turn over! Clay was climbing out of his SUV, parked ahead of her. Valerie desperately tried to pick the best escape route. It was dark on the shoulder of the road. If he smashed her window, he could easily get into the car. But if she jumped out of the car—and began to scream and run at the same time—maybe she could reach the crowd of people at the door of the restaurant.

Valerie threw open the door and leaped out. She ran for the restaurant, yelling as loud as she could. But Clay moved with the speed of a wildcat. In a second he grabbed her shoulders and spun her around.

"Help!" Valerie screamed, looking desperately at the people who seemed to be so near. But loud music was blaring from several of the parked cars, and nobody heard her. Everybody was too busy having a good time.

Valerie knew the police would be there any minute. Please hurry! she silently pleaded.

■ ■ ■

Clay threw Valerie into the SUV and took off. "The police are on their way," Valerie told him. "It's all over, Clay—don't make it any worse!"

"But we *won't* be here," Clay said as he turned down a dark country road. Then he accelerated to 80 miles an hour, and Valerie's hands tightened into bloodless fists.

"Clay, the police are coming! *Don't!"* Valerie pleaded.

Clay Turman glanced at her, his face disfigured with rage. "You know where we're going, baby? We're going the back way into Cougar Canyon. You remember

Cougar Canyon, don't you? Only this time you won't be *dreaming* about seeing a guy carrying a body!"

A shudder went through Valerie's heart. Even if the police were swarming over the interstate, how would they know Clay had taken this road? When they eventually did pick up the trail, it could very well be too late.

"Know what happened, baby? Might as well tell you now. I spotted Bonnie Lewis when we were in Skippy's. You were swilling a Manhattan, so I went over to kid with her. She brushed me off, as usual. Then I saw her again in the parking lot. Since there was nobody around, I slapped her across her stupid face. She came at me like a wildcat. I was so mad I got my hands around her neck and squeezed. I didn't even know what I was doing until she went limp. I didn't know what else to do, so I stuck her in the trunk. Then I went back in to get you. I got you another mixed drink, a double. You barely made it to the car. But you woke up in the mountains, I guess. You woke up just long enough to spoil everything for both of us," Clay said bitterly.

Valerie's heart pounded in terror as the SUV climbed the mountain road. The police would never track them here. But then, in the distance, she heard the whine of sirens. Her heart leaped with hope. They must be sending cruisers up and down every road in the area!

A wild look of hate came over Clay's face. He increased his speed, skidding around every bend in the road. Then, finally, he swerved down a narrow dirt road leading off the asphalt. The SUV bounced to a stop in a stand of fir trees. "Come on, we're heading into the woods," Clay said, "and we're going on foot. They're never going to take me—not as long as I've got you as a hostage!"

■ ■ ■

Valerie looked around in panic. Then she saw something out of the corner of her eye. The tip of the iron steering wheel guard—the iron bar Clay said she had used to kill Bonnie—was sticking out from under the seat! Valerie waited until Clay turned his back. Then she reached down and grabbed the bar. Grasping it with both hands, she brought it crashing down on Clay's head. She'd caught him by surprise! He let out a loud shriek of pain and tumbled backward, blood running from his head.

Valerie jumped out of the SUV and ran back toward the highway. She felt sick. When she saw a small stream, she paused to throw cold water on her face so she wouldn't faint. The cold water revived her enough to keep on running.

When the first police car approached, Valerie flagged it down with waving arms. "I've killed Clay Turman!" she cried. "He was going to kill me!"

A few minutes later an ambulance pulled up. The paramedics told Valerie that Clay Turman had a concussion but was far from dead. Valerie got into one of the police cruisers and was taken directly to the police station to tell her story. Brad Duncan was waiting for her there. And although he was only a good friend and not a boyfriend—at least not yet—he took the crying girl in his arms and held her for a good long time.

For Valerie, the very bad dream was finally over.

After-Reading Wrap-Up

1. Is *The Very Bad Dream* a good title for the story? Why or why not? Think of another title for the story.

2. Reread the scenes in the book that include Amy. Why do you think the author created this character?

3. When did you first think that Clay might be the murderer? Write down what Clay said or did that made you suspect him.

4. What did you think of Valerie? Can you see any similarities between her and yourself? Explain.

5. At first, Valerie thought her dream was triggered by a news report on the radio. What changed her mind?

6. Clay might have gotten away with murder if it hadn't been for Valerie. What was the first thing she did that spoiled his plans?